Bear's Best Friend

Lucy Coats and Sarah Dyer

BLOOMSBURY

LONDON   NEW DELHI   NEW YORK   SYDNEY

Bear has lots of friends . . .

. . . but he doesn't have a BEST FRIEND.

EVERYONE has a best friend but Bear.

Squirrel has Mole . . .

Rabbit has Frog . . .

and Deer has Hedgehog.

But WHO could be the best friend for a bear who loves to make tree pictures?

Bear makes a special tree picture
for each of his friends.

Maybe that will help him to have a proper think.
Bear wonders and wonders while he clippety-clips.

Would Hedgehog be too spiny?

Would Rabbit be
too loppity?

Deer too spiky?

Mole might be
too velvety.

Squirrel too flippy-floppy . . .

and would Frog be just
too hoppity to hug?

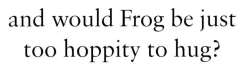

All Bear's friends like their tree pictures A LOT.

They give a party so that all the other animals can see them.

Soon everyone in the forest wants a tree picture of their very own.

Here's Fox . . .

Here's Duck . . .

Here's Otter . . .

And here's Owl.

Bear is busier than a buzzy bee, but he STILL hasn't found his best friend.

Bear sighs a big bear sigh.

Surely his best friend must be SOMEWHERE in the forest.

Soon Bear is sad.

Three big fat tears fall on to his snipping scissors.

SPLIT!

SPLAT!

SPLOT!

Then Bear hears a tiny whisper. He turns round.

"Why are you crying, Bear?" says a shy little voice.

It's **another** bear!

A bear with **hair**.

Twirly,

swirly,

curly,

cuddly,

huggly,

snuggly hair.

A BEST FRIEND sort of bear,
with BEST FRIEND sort of hair!

A note about Bear's Tree Pictures:

Bear's favourite activity is snipping and clipping trees
into marvellous shapes with his sharp snickety shears.
This has a special name all of its own,
and is called topiary.